The Adventures of Roman

The Adventures of Roman German is a digital and hardcover children's entertainment experience. Roman German and his friends, Matt-the-Monkey and Jerry-the Giraffe, are searching the world for hidden pieces of technology. Join them as they piece the device together and uncover the mysterious messages being transmitted to his guardian: Rob the Robot.

Chapter 1

Roman German is an adventurous boy with some incredible friends. Matt-the-Monkey is a math wiz who loves creating and playing video games. Rob-the-Robot has the most advanced computer brain in the world. Jerry-the-Giraffe, well, Jerry loves coconuts!

The Blue Mountains

Every day after school, they all meet at the clubhouse that Roman and his dad built together. It is full of gadgets, games and delicious snacks. It's also the place they plan all of their adventures. Today, they decided to travel to the Blue Mountains, a beautiful collection of forests, cliffs and all sorts of animals.

As they began their trip, they heard a rustling noise. Was it a giant koala? Was it a slithering snake? Was it only just the wind? They each took guesses as to what it could be.

A Big Hole!

While they made their way up the mountain, suddenly, Matt fell into a deep hole. There were rocks and sticks and bugs crawling all around.

"Help!", he yelled, "these bugs are tickling my toes!"

Rob Pulled Him Out!

Roman spotted a vine high up in a nearby tree. Jerry grabbed Rob and swung him into the tree with his long neck. Rob untangled the vine and threw it down to Matt. "Time to leave these bugs behind", Matt said, and Rob pulled him out with his robot strength.

When they looked around, they found holes everywhere, each one with leaves on top of them. "Who dug all these holes?", they wondered.

As they continued along the trail, they ran across a Park Ranger with a giant shovel. Roman asked the Ranger, "why are there so many holes along the trail?"

"Well", the Ranger said, "you must have missed the 'trail closed' sign. We have had a number of giant lizard sightings up here, so we laid a few traps."

Trail Closed Sign
TRAIL
CLOSED

"Giant Lizard!!"

"GIANT LIZARD!!", they all exclaimed. "Yes", he said, "when he's looking for a tasty snack, he runs through the mountains lightning fast. People say it sounds like the wind in the trees".

They all looked at each other with big wide eyes. "Yikes", said Roman, "I think that's enough hiking for one day." So they packed up and took off back to the clubhouse.

Chapter 2

"Little Collins Beach"

The next day, Roman and his friends traveled to Little Collins Beach. It was Roman's favourite because it was surrounded by a forest, had a waterfall and a perfect spot for cliff-jumping. They had been drawn there because Rob was picking up a mysterious signal buried deep within the sand.

When they arrived, they could all hear a muffled noise coming from a pile of sand. **bwaa-bwaap... bwaa-bwaap**. The signal kept repeating and grew louder as they each took turns digging in the sand. Well, everyone except Jerry. Instead, Jerry just went searching for coconuts. Jerry LOVES coconuts!

Jerry Loves Coconuts

Sure enough, they found the device that was making the sound. As soon as it came out of the sand, Rob started to zing and pop and swirl around. Everyone looked at him and exclaimed "WHAT IS HAPPENING??!!"

"I don't know", Rob said, "let's bring this thing with us so we can investigate".

The Club House!

By the time they arrived at the clubhouse, Rob had already learned a great deal about it. He informed the friends that the device they found was one of many pieces hidden all over the earth. They were each sent by an astronaut who is currently in another galaxy. Each piece was to remain hidden until he truly needed help.

Now the time had come and Roman knew he and his friends were at the beginning of their greatest adventure.

Another Galaxy

“The Trip to Macazanium”

While Roman and his friends waited for Rob to figure out where the next piece was hidden, they decided to investigate the first piece they found. They looked at it from every angle. They put it under a bright light, they dunked it in water and even tried to connect it to some electricity. But nothing seemed to work.

“Aha!”, Matt said, “My sister Mary is a techno-archeologist, let’s bring it to her.”

Chapter 3

The Trip to Macazanium Cave

When they arrived at Mary's clubhouse, they quickly realised she was gone. However, Mibo7, the robot she built, was still there.

Matt asked Mibo7, "Where did Mary go?". Beep-boop-beep "Mary has traveled to the Macazanium Bat Caves, she is on a scientific mission", Mibo7 said. "I will send the map of the caves to Rob," beep-boop-beep.

As soon as they returned home, Roman asked his parents if they could have a ride to the Macazanium bat caves. "Of course", Roman's dad said, "but you will have to wait awhile because the car is downloading an upgrade. If you have another way to get to the caves, you can go, as long as you all stick together."

Car Downloading an upgrade

Well, this would mean they had to create their own transportation. They brought all of their bikes together, found old mechanical parts in Roman's garage and Rob pieced together a giant sail from old blankets, clothes and fishing wire. When it was finished, Roman, Matt and Jerry could each pedal-power the new machine while Rob caught the wind and attached the sail to the front of the contraption.

While they were on their way, the wind started to get stronger and stronger. It pulled so hard on the sail that the friends didn't need to peddle at all. Faster and faster they went, thankfully they built in seatbelts for each rider. Up ahead, they saw a huge tree that was bent over onto the sidewalk.

Bikes Together

They tried to avoid it but the wind crashed them right into the tree. The only problem was, when they crashed, it caused the bent over tree to spring back up, launching everything and everyone straight into the sky. It looked like it was raining bicycles.

Huge Tree Bent Over

Rob zipped around and turned the sail into a parachute. As they returned from the sky, they found themselves gliding in the air, positioned perfectly to drop right at the entrance to the Macazanium Bat Caves.

When they landed, they packed away the parachute and ate a quick snack, getting ready for the journey deep underground. The moment they entered the cave, they all stared as Rob started to zing and pop and swirl around.

Deep Underground

Made in the USA
Middletown, DE
21 January 2022